Footprints on the Moon

Poems About Space

Lee Aucoin, *Creative Director*
Jamey Acosta, *Senior Editor*
Heidi Fiedler, *Editor*
Produced and designed by
Denise Ryan & Associates
Illustration © Helen Poole
Rachelle Cracchiolo, *Publisher*

Teacher Created Materials
5301 Oceanus Drive
Huntington Beach, CA 92649-1030
http://www.tcmpub.com
Paperback: ISBN: 978-1-4333-5564-6
Library Binding: ISBN: 978-1-4807-1709-1
© 2014 Teacher Created Materials
Made in China
Nordica.122017.CA21701269

Selected by
Mark Carthew

Illustrated by
Helen Poole

Contents

Space Counting Rhyme

10 flying saucers, 10 flashing lights

9 glowing trails, 9 meteorites

8 silver spaceships trying hard

to find

7 lost aliens left behind

6 burning comets blazing fire

5 red rockets blasting higher

4 satellites, 4 radar dishes

3 stars shooting, means 3 wishes

2 bright lights – the moon and sun

1 little me to shine upon

Paul Cookson

It's Hard to Count Stars

One

Two

Three

Four

Have I counted you before?

Four

Five

Six

Ten

Perhaps I should begin again.

Philip Burton

Brief Encounter

Zooming on and on

Through space,

I want to see

a Martian's face,

And when I've said,

"Hallo", well then

I want to zoom

Back home again.

Clive Webster

Fly Me to the Moon

I've built a big blue rocket ship
with silver stars and stripes.
It flies me to the yellow moon
and through the dark black night.
10, 9, 8, 7, 6, 5, 4, 3, 2, 1, 0
Blast off!

Mark Carthew

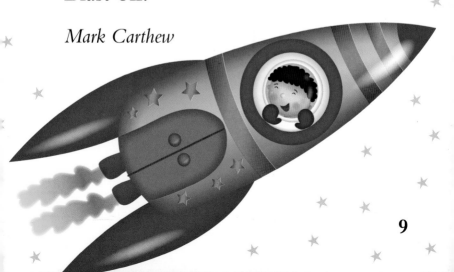

Footprints on the Moon

There were men on the moon once.
They traveled through space
and found that the moon
was a dry, dusty place.

They collected some moon rocks
and had a look round
and left lots of footprints
there on the ground.

They couldn't stay long
as the moon has no air,
but the footprints they left
in the dust are still there.

Marion Swinger

Moon, Moon

Moon, Moon, up in the sky
how long have you been shining?
And what's beneath your surface
and crusty crater lining?
There are so many questions
in your moonlit face,
shining down upon the Earth
and into outer space.

Mark Carthew

Mars

Mars is red,
And Mars is rusty,
Sandy, rocky,
Very dusty.

Mars has ice caps.
Once had streams.
Mars has Martians...
In your dreams!

Douglas Florian

13

When I Am an Astronaut

First I'll get into my spacesuit.
Then I'll bravely wave good-by.
Next I'll climb into my spacecraft
Built to sail right through the sky!
In command inside the capsule,
I will talk to ground control.
When we've checked out
all the systems,
I'll say, "Let the countdown roll!"
And it's 4-3-2-1 - - blast off - -
With a smile upon my face,
I'll spin loops around the planets
up, up, up in outer space!

Bobbi Katz

Zoom, Zoom, Zoom

Zoom, Zoom, Zoom,
We're going to the moon.

Zoom, Zoom, Zoom,
We're going to the moon.

If you want to take a trip,
Climb aboard my rocket ship.

Zoom, Zoom, Zoom,
We're going to the moon.

Five, four, three, two, one:
Blast off!

Traditional

16

Meteors

They hurtle through space
at a very fast pace
tracing old orbits and trails.

In a wink of eye
they shoot along by
showing glimpses of star–dusty tails.

They zip
and they zoom
past the Earth and the moon
like fireflies dancing at night.

I look up and stare
just wondering where
I might see one later tonight.

Mark Carthew

The Alien

The Alien
Was as round as the moon.
Five legs he had
And his ears played a tune.
His hair was pink
And his knees were green,
He was the funniest thing I'd seen.
As he danced in the door
Of his strange space craft.
He looked at me –
And laughed and laughed!

Julie Holder

Blast Off

A rocket ship
will take you far
to see a crater,
quasar,
star,
constellations - -
            brilliant, bright - -
a planet,
comet,
meteorite - -

Blast off, child,
it's
time
for
flight.

Lee Bennett Hopkins

Space Riddle

Flies down low
with a shimmering glow.
From where they come
we do not know.

Mark Carthew

Solar System Show

The solar system is much bigger
than Mercury, Venus, Mars.
Bigger still than all of Earth
the sun, the moon and stars.

Jupiter's moons, Saturn's rings,
and galaxies that glow
are all just little pieces
of the solar system show.

There's asteroids the size of states,
ice planets tht shine bright;
Solar winds and big gas clouds,
black holes as black as night.

A 100 million comets and much
more that we don't know;
A starry feast all sparkling
in an interstellar show.

Mark Carthew

25

Star Light, Star Bright

Star light,
Star bright,
First star I see tonight,
I wish I may,
I wish I might
Have the wish
I wish tonight.

Traditional

Sources and Acknowledgments

Burton, Philip. "It's Hard to Count the Stars" from *Space Poems*. London: Macmillan Children's Books, 2006. Reprinted by permission of Macmillan Children's Books, London.

Carthew, Mark. "Fly Me to the Moon," "Meteors," "Moon, Moon," "Solar System Show," and "Space Riddle." Published by permission of the author.

Cookson, Paul. "Space Counting Rhyme" from *Space Poems*. London: Macmillan Children's Books, 2006. Reprinted by permission of Macmillan Children's Books, London.

Florien, Douglas. "Mars" from *Comets, Stars, the Moon and Mars: Space Poems and Paintings*. Orlando: Harcourt, 2007. Reprinted by permission of Harcourt, Orlando.

Holder, Julie "The Alien" from *Poems about Space*. East Sussex: Wayland Publishers Ltd, 1999. Reprinted by permission of Wayland Publishers Ltd, Hove, East Sussex.

Hopkins, Lee Bennett. "Blast Off!" from *Blast Off! Poems about Space*. New York: Harper Collins, 1995. Reprinted by permission of Harper Collins, New York.

Katz, Bobbi. "When I Am an Astronaut" from *Blast Off! Poems About Space*. New York: Harper Collins, 1995. Reprinted by permission of Harper Collins, New York.

Swinger, Marion. "Footprints on the Moon" from *Space Poems*. London: Macmillan Children's Books, 2006. Reprinted by permission of Macmillan Children's Books, London.

Webster, Clive. "Brief Encounter" from *Poems about Space*. East Sussex: Wayland Publishers Ltd, 1999. Reprinted by permission of Wayland Publishers Ltd, Hove, East Sussex.

Every effort has been made to trace and acknowledge copyright. The publishers welcome information that would rectify any error or omissions in subsequent editions.